*To Balqees Ul-Hassan, with grateful thanks*

Text copyright © Franzeska G. Ewart 2007
Illustrations copyright © Helen Bate 2007
The right of Franzeska G. Ewart to be identified as the author
and of Helen Bate to be identified as the illustrator of this work
has been asserted by them in accordance with the Copyright,
Designs and Patents Act, 1988 (United Kingdom).

First published in Great Britain in 2007 and in the USA in 2008 by
Frances Lincoln Children's Books, 4 Torriano Mews,
Torriano Avenue, London NW5 2RZ
www.franceslincoln.com

This edition published in Great Britain and in the USA in 2012

A catalogue record for this book is available from the British Library.

ISBN 978-1-84780-330-6

Printed and bound by CPI Group (UK) Ltd, Croydon, CR0 4YY in January 2012

1 3 5 7 9 8 6 4 2

# Sita, Snake-Queen of Speed

## Franzeska G. Ewart

*Illustrated by* Helen Bate

# The Thrill Ride to End All Thrill Rides

There's a feeling I get when I'm excited – I wonder if you've ever had it?

It's like an electric current rushing up my back, and when it reaches my head it makes my face go hot, and it feels as if my hair is standing on end. It only happens when I'm really excited, and it happened the very moment I heard about Sita, Snake-Queen of Speed.

Even the name thrilled me through and through, but there was more. For Sita, Snake-Queen of Speed had a Thrill Ride the likes of which I'd never dreamt about, not even in my wildest dreams.

It was my best friend Kylie Teasdale who told me about it, and, even before she'd finished telling me, I knew I had to see Sita for myself. Not just see her. I knew I had to ride with her on the Thrill Ride to end all Thrill Rides.

That was tricky though, because Sita, Snake-Queen of Speed was one of the rides at Thrill City. And unfortunately, Thrill City is not the kind of place my family (that's Mum, and Dad, and Nani, and Bilal, my baby brother) would ever go for a holiday.

Bradford – yes. Thrill City – no.

Anyway, Kylie told me about Sita and her amazing Snake Ride after she came back from Thrill City in the Spring Holidays. She talked about nothing else for four entire days.

"It's fabulous, Yosser," she said, as we waited for the morning bell to ring. "Utterly, mind-blowingly, fabulous."

By the way, Kylie says she gets the electric-current thing up her back too, and her hair feels like it's standing on end. And since Kylie's mum lets her get her hair streaked yellow and orange and red, it's a real shame that it doesn't really stand on end – because how cool would that be!

Kylie's mum also let Kylie get her tummy button pierced. I once asked my mum if I could get my tummy button pierced and she said – 'Not while I have breath in my body and blood in my veins'. Which is her way of saying no.

Kylie's great at describing things. She uses such good words that she makes pictures appear in your mind. One day she's going to be a famous writer, but for the time being she's practising on me.

So I shut my eyes and listened to Kylie telling me about Sita, Snake-Queen of Speed, and the more she told me, the more I pictured her. And the more I pictured her, the more I knew I had to go to Thrill City.

"You get strapped into this thing called a Snake Pod," Kylie explained. "The outside's painted to look like snakeskin, and the front is a snake's head.

"Even the seats are snakeskin," she went on, "and the bit you hold on to is…" Kylie paused and took a big breath, "… a blood-stained fang."

I shivered. I wanted to ask Kylie if the fang was actually wet and sticky with blood. I didn't though, because I knew deep down they wouldn't be allowed real blood; in fact, they probably wouldn't be allowed even wet and sticky fake blood.

"Right ahead of you," Kylie went on, "there's this

huge model of Sita, and you have never in your life seen anyone so *cooool*. She's got green snakeskin boots, and green snakeskin gloves, and round her neck she has a little golden snake. Her eyes are yellow, and her hair is long and black and..." Kylie clutched my arm hard, "... there are snakes writhing about in it!"

"Oh my goodness!" I breathed. "But not really writhing?"

I couldn't believe they'd really writhe – like, actually move back and forth and from side to side.

Kylie was nodding though. "The model's a kind of Virtual Reality computer thing," she said, "so Sita walks about..."

"... and the snakes writhe?" I said, just to make quite sure.

Kylie nodded. "Writhe like anything! Sometimes, a snake'll writhe down towards you and open its jaws, so you can see its forked tongue and its fangs."

"Does deadly venom drip from the fangs, Kylie?" I asked.

I know quite a lot about snakes, you see, because I've got snakes at home, though they're not alive. They belong to my nani and they're stuffed, like a lot of Nani's things. She's got a huge collection, mostly birds and lizards, which she keeps in her bedroom.

Nani knows all about snakes, which is how I know

that snakes' fangs are hollow, and they inject deadly venom through them into their prey.

"Deadly venom and blood, Yosser," nodded Kylie. "It's awesome."

She didn't have to tell me. I had the clearest picture of Sita, Snake-Queen of Speed inside my head.

And it had *awesome* written all over it.

# A Truly Massive G-Force

It was nearly time for the bell to ring, but Kylie hadn't finished describing Sita, Snake-Queen of Speed and her amazing Thrill Ride.

"Then there's a really loud hiss," she said, "and the Snake Pod tips forward so you're hanging upside down. All the blood rushes to your head and you can hear your heart beating in your ears!"

I bent over and stuck my head between my knees to see if I could hear my heart beating in my ears. The blood certainly rushed to my head. Then there was a high-pitched buzzing sound, and for a moment I thought my ear-drums had burst. Then I realised it was just the bell.

"Then this incredible hi-i-i-i-s-s-s-s-s-y voice booms out," Kylie said, as we lined up to go in, "and it says *I am S-s-s-s-s-s-s-s-sita, S-s-s-s-s-s-s-s-s-s snake-Queen of S-s-s-s-s-s-s-s-s-s-speed. Do you dare to ride with me?*'"

Kylie's great at voices. She made Sita's voice hiss like anything. In fact, she hissed saliva all over my face.

"What if you didn't?" I asked.

"Didn't what?"

"Dare to ride with her?" I said.

Kylie gave a snort. "It'd be a bit late to decide you didn't dare when they'd strapped you in and hung you upside down. And anyway," she gave another snort, "anyone who's chicken doesn't go to Thrill City."

Now, I know Kylie wasn't meaning to suggest for a moment that I was chicken. It's not something Kylie

11

would do. But all the same, it made me even more determined to go, just to prove to myself I wasn't.

Ms Albright, our teacher, was standing in front of the school door, staring out towards the football pitch, looking for stragglers. She always did that, and it was great because, if you were lucky, you could manage another good five-minutes' worth of chat while she shouted at them.

"So then what happens?" I whispered, keeping my mouth rigid. Ms Albright's hawk-eyes could spot your lips moving a mile off.

"Sita does a countdown to ten," Kylie whispered back, "and everybody joins in, and when you get to *eight* you feel a judder and on *nine* the Snake Pod starts to move, and..."

"On *ten* you're off?" I said.

"You never get to hear *ten*," Kylie whispered, "because a Truly Massive G-Force shoots you into Sita's Snake-Kingdom."

She paused dramatically.

"What's a Truly Massive G-Force?" I asked.

Kylie thought about it for a while.

"That's what it said on the brochure," she said finally.

Ms Albright was holding a football above her head and telling our class to *walk smartly in*. I sneaked a glance at Kylie. She was still thinking hard.

"Truly Massive G-Forces are hard to explain," she muttered as we passed Ms Albright.

"Try," I said.

"Lips," said Ms Albright. She raised her eyebrows pointedly at us, and we marched silently in.

Even when we were half-way down the corridor, Kylie still didn't dare try to explain the G-Force thing. When Ms Albright said *lips*, she meant *lips*.

Actually, I was pretty sure Kylie didn't have the first clue what a Truly Massive G-Force was. Which was a bit of a let-down, because I really wanted to know what it looked like, and whether it had snakes dangling from it.

And I wasn't sure even my nani would know that.

# The Fly In The Ointment

At this point I have to put Sita, Snake-Queen of Speed and the Truly Massive G-Force on hold, because there's something else you need to know.

It's what my dad calls a *fly in the ointment* – the *ointment* being your life, and the *fly* being something that utterly ruins it. And the fly in my particular ointment that summer was Our Lady of the Sorrows.

My mum and dad, you see, had always had a bee in their bonnet about me going to a private school when I left Primary. They said a private school, with just girls, would be 'much more conducive to study' than the local comprehensive and, after surfing the Net and examining every league table under the sun, they'd hit on Our Lady as the best school in the area. So off we went, my mum and my dad and me, to see it. (Nani stayed at home to look after Bilal and make sure he didn't eat the furniture.)

When I first walked into Our Lady of the Sorrows, I must admit I liked the atmosphere. OK, there were statues everywhere, but they had lovely faces, so I knew I'd get used to them. And it was really quiet and calm – not like our school at all.

But it was when we were in the Head's office that the bee in Mum and Dad's bonnet began to turn into a horrible buzzy fly in my ointment. It began to turn, in fact, the very moment I set eyes on Sister Mary Ignatius.

It wasn't that Sister Mary Ignatius was huge and scary-looking. Not a bit of it. She was shorter than me, and her face reminded me of Nani's stuffed canary with a little hooked beak, and a neat grey veil in place of yellow feathers. But there was something about her eyes and the determined way she said, *We'll make a first-rate scholar out of Yosser if it's the last thing we do…* that made a horrible stomach-curdling feeling of dread wash over me.

Sister Mary Ignatius's eyes were black and sparkly, and the lenses in her glasses were so strong they made her eyes look absolutely enormous.

That was a bit scary, but not nearly as scary as her voice. It was very quiet indeed, but it had that edge to it that let you know she'd get her own way no matter what. And when she listed all the school rules (of which there were about ten million) she kept turning to me and

15

giving me that ultrasonic stare as though she thought I'd be breaking every one of them as soon as I crossed the threshold.

Finally, at rule number nine million nine thousand nine hundred and ninety-nine (*School uniform must be worn at all times*) she leaned over her desk, glared at me with her huge eyes, and sniffed.

"Positively no jeans," she said, aiming the sniff in the general direction of my legs. I was about to point out that actually they weren't jeans, they were combats, but one look at Sister Mary Ignatius's eyes and I decided an in-depth discussion of fashion was not appropriate. I just bit my lip and shook my head, as though I'd never really liked combats anyway.

But I was truly miserable. I'd seen some girls as we came in, all identically dressed in bright green jumpers. Some had jaunty tartan skirts and neat black stockings, and others had jaunty tartan trousers, and at the time I'd thought they looked quite cool. Now it was beginning to dawn on me that I could be one of those girls, and that Sister Mary Ignatius and her teachers could be making a first-rate scholar out of me for the next six years ...

And in that moment I realised I didn't want to be at Our Lady of the Sorrows at all.

Not without Kylie.

I looked pleadingly at Mum, but she and Dad were shaking Sister Mary Ignatius's hand, and they were all smiling happily.

"Good day to you, Mr Farooq," Sister Mary was saying in a business-like voice, "and we look forward to seeing Yosser in the very near future, for her entrance exam ..."

That did it. I didn't think I could feel worse, but I instantly did.

Entrance exam. The words were like a great bell booming out my fate, as Kylie put it when I told her later. And as usual, Kylie was spot-on.

I've always been terrified of exams, you see. Even Ms Albright's regular Friday Mental Maths and Spelling combo used make me feel sick. The thought of sitting an exam in Our Lady of the Sorrows' big hall was more than I could stand.

As soon as we were outside, I told Mum and Dad I didn't want to go, but I could see there was absolutely no point. They were hooked. They thought Our Lady of the Sorrows was perfect and Sister Mary Ignatius was wonderful.

"I could see the way she was looking at you, Yosser," Mum said, her eyes moist with happiness. "She was looking right in at your Hidden Potential..."

"... and planning how to unleash it," added Dad, smacking his lips as though my Hidden Potential was a tasty meal. "Our Lady of the Sorrows will be the making of you, Yosser. You mark my words."

I clambered miserably into the car, took out my mobile, and texted Kylie to tell her what had happened. Then I sat in silence all the way home, thinking about my fate, and even Kylie texting back a smily-face didn't cheer me up.

# A Fearless Band of Snake-Warriors

"Nani," I asked, "what's a Truly Massive G-Force?"

Mum and Nani and Bilal and I were sitting round the table, having tea. Dad wasn't there, because he always works very late in our shop (which is called Farooq's Fruits). Mum and Nani and I were eating chicken pakora. Bilal was eating the tablecloth.

Nani rolled her tongue round her mouth several times, which is what she does when she's thinking. "I think it's a kind of underwear..." she said at last, but I could see she wasn't sure.

"I don't think it can be, Nani-jee," I said as politely as I could. "Because Kylie says it shoots you into Sita's Snake Kingdom. Underwear couldn't do that."

We went on eating in silence for a while. I tried to stop myself imagining a huge pair of pants pushing a Snake Pod along a track. Then I took a big breath in, gritted my teeth, and asked:

"Can I go to Thrill City this summer? Please?"

Mum and Nani looked at me with puzzled expressions. Bilal spat the tablecloth out.

I explained in vivid detail all about Thrill City, and how cool it was, and how everybody goes there, and when I'd finished Mum said, like I knew she would, "Wait till your Dad gets home, Yosser, but the answer's probably 'No'. It would cost too much and anyway, we always go to Auntie Rosina's in Bradford."

A big lump filled my throat then, and my eyes went prickly. I knew there was no point saying anything more till Dad was there, so I went to my bedroom, where I lay on my bed and made two mental lists: one of my chances of getting Dad to agree, and the other of my chances of not getting Dad to agree.

The second list went on and on … and the first item on it was, *Think how much money we'll be spending on you if you pass the entrance exam for Our Lady of the Sorrows.*

I couldn't think of a single item for the first list.

To take my mind off it I drew the best picture of Sita I could, remembering Kylie's brilliant description. I drew her in a short dress made of red and yellow flames, and I gave her green snakeskin boots and green snakeskin gloves, and masses of snakes writhing about in her hair, and a little golden snake round her neck.

In the background I drew a Snake Pod, with a glistening-red fang to hold on to, and then I drew myself, strapped down in the Pod, waiting for countdown.

I decided to miss out the Truly Massive G-Force till I knew what it was.

Then I pinned the picture above my bed and lay down and looked up at it, trying to think what Sita would do if she wanted something very, very much. Sita wouldn't lie on her bed and cry, I was sure of that. She wouldn't throw a temper tantrum either. What would she do?

I was racking my brains when there was a tap at my door and Nani poked her head in. "Yosser," she said softly. "I have something to show you – may I come in?"

"Sure, Nani-jee," I said, and she sat beside me with the thing she had to show me on her lap. It was a funny shape, and it was covered in a large woollen vest.

"How much does this Thrill City cost, Yosser?" Nani asked.

She'd spotted the picture of Sita, and I could see from the sparkle in her eyes that she liked her a lot.

"Loads," I said. "Over a hundred pounds, I bet."

I couldn't keep my eyes off the thing on Nani's lap. "What's that, Nani-jee?" I said, and Nani pulled the vest off. It was a stuffed weasely thing with black glass eyes and sharp teeth, and the teeth were sunk into a stuffed cobra which was all coiled round it.

"It's a mongoose killing a cobra," Nani said proudly. "Nanoo gave it to me as an engagement present. He was always very romantic ..."

She stood up and put the stuffed mongoose on the shelf above my bed, beside the picture of Sita. "Great little fighters, mongooses are," she said, admiringly. "Specially where snakes are concerned."

"Is it for me?" I asked. I wasn't sure I wanted the mongoose and the cobra in my bedroom. Sometimes Nani's stuffed things get wood weavels, because they've got sawdust inside. And they smell of mothballs, but underneath the mothball smell there's another smell, which I don't entirely trust.

Nani nodded. "Thought you'd like it," she said. "Because of the cobra."

I thanked her and decided it was a nice thing to have in my bedroom after all, because it went so well with the Sita picture.

"Thrill City sounds wonderful," Nani said then, and suddenly I felt a tiny flicker of electric current at the bottom of my spine.

It got stronger when she said the next thing though.

"Supposing we went together, Yosser?"

I nodded like mad. Then I remembered. "But neither of us has any money, Nani-jee," I said. "And if I pass the entrance exam, Our Lady of the Sorrows'll be taking all Dad's."

Nani stood up, rather creakily. "We don't need to go for long, do we?" she said. "Just long enough to ride with Sita…"

"Of course!" I said. "One night would do it. But the money?"

Nani ran her tongue round her mouth thoughtfully.

When she spoke again, her voice was very determined.

"I'll speak to your dad," she said. "Maybe if I told him you were going to earn some of the money?"

She gave my arm a little punch with her fist. "You know what your dad's always saying, Yosser," she reminded me. *"Look after the pennies, and the pounds will look after themselves."*

Then she jabbed her thumb up towards Sita, Snake-Queen of Speed. "Come on," she said. "You've got to do it – for Sita!" And then she headed off downstairs to wait for Dad to come home.

I lay back on my bed and wracked my brains to think of a way to earn some money, and I must have fallen asleep. Then a little miracle happened. When I woke up it was almost dark, and the first things I saw were the ghostly shadows of Sita and the mongoose – and, believe it or not, I knew just what to do.

I knew what to do, because suddenly I knew what Sita would do, if she was strapped for cash. It was obvious, really. She'd gather a Fearless Band of Snake-Warriors around her, and they'd hunt for treasure! They'd borrow their dad's metal detector, and they'd scour the countryside. They'd leave no stone unturned, and they'd face every danger with courage, till they found the treasure that would bring them their hearts' desire.

And that was what we had to do too.

I took my mobile out of my pocket and hit the 'txt' button. I couldn't wait to tell Kylie.

# A Treasure Quest

Next day was Saturday and, first thing in the morning, Kylie came round to my house with a carrier bag which she tipped on to my bed.

"Here we are," she said. "Everything a Fearless Band of Snake-Warriors could possibly need!"

"Wow," I said, quietly.

I said it quietly because, to be honest, Kylie's Snake-Warrior Equipment didn't have a huge wow-factor. It was two rubber snakes, one green and one yellow, and two pairs of rubber gloves, one pink and one blue.

"What do you think?" she said. "I know the gloves aren't the right colour for snakeskin but I thought they'd do. We've got tons of rubber gloves in our house. On account of my dad's ferrets."

"Your dad's got ferrets?" I asked.

"Sure," said Kylie. "Champion ferrets. Won Best of Breed in the Angora Class last year, he did. This year he's dead set on getting Best In Show."

Kylie's dad was a man of few words. Every time I went to Kylie's house he was out the back, in what I'd assumed was his potting-shed, but now realised must be his ferret-shed. Suddenly I wanted to know all about it, but then I thought we shouldn't really hang around talking ferrets when there was treasure to be found, so I made Kylie promise to tell me more later on. Then I pulled on the pink rubber gloves.

"You can have the yellow snake round your neck, because it's more like gold," Kylie said generously.

That really made my day. "Does that mean I'm Sita?" I said, and Kylie nodded.

"I'm your Humble Vassal," she said and, because I must have looked puzzled, she explained that a vassal was a sort of servant.

"I will be at your beck and call at all times, noble Sita," she said humbly, and she bowed and pulled on the blue rubber gloves and knotted the green rubber snake loosely round her neck.

She picked up the metal detector (I'd decided Dad wouldn't mind if I took it without asking, since it was a good cause) and hoisted it on to her shoulder.

"Do I look fearless?" she asked, and I nodded and knotted the yellow rubber snake round my neck.

Then we faced my Sita-picture, and we thumped the snakes round our necks first with one snakeskin-clad hand and then with the other, like a special Snake-Warrior salute.

It made us both feel very brave.

"OK," I said. "So what do we do now?"

"I suppose," Kylie said, "we start scouring the countryside for treasure."

"A Treasure Quest?" I said, and Kylie nodded.

And that's what we did. A Treasure Quest. All morning.

We started off in the park. We took it in turns to wave the metal detector from side to side over the long grass, and it blipped loads of times, which was really exciting. But when we searched through the grass it was always a ring-pull we found, or a beer can, or a rusty old nail.

Once, Kylie found a two pence coin, which cheered us up no end. But after that it was more ring-pulls and nails, and we began to lose heart; so we decided to try our luck in the town.

We got a few odd looks as we marched along Little Malden High Street in our Snake-Warrior outfits, but we ignored them. The metal detector battery was running out by then, so we stopped using it and just walked with our heads down, eyes glued to the pavement, but we didn't find a thing.

Once, I spotted what might have been an ancient Treasure Map. It was a piece of yellowy paper covered in spidery handwriting, and it was stuck to the pavement with some chewing gum.

Peeling it off was not a pleasant task (and best done

by a Humble Vassal) but when Kylie managed to open it up and read the ancient spidery handwriting, all it said was:

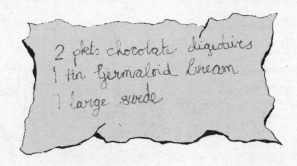

2 pkts chocolate digestives
1 tin Germaloid Cream
1 large swede

…which was a Bitter Disappointment.

Feeling very dejected, we sat on the Post Office windowsill and took off our rubber gloves for a scratch. Rubber gloves get very clammy, especially when it's hot. I bet snakeskin's better. I bet Sita doesn't sweat.

"I don't think there's any treasure in Little Malden, Yosser," Kylie said at last, taking the two pence coin out of her pocket and looking at it dismally.

She was wrong, though. There was treasure in Little Malden. But it wasn't at all the kind of treasure we'd been thinking of. And we had a few more trials to go through before we found it.

We'd just decided to go home and watch cartoons and forget the Treasure Quest, when who should come out of the Post Office but Nani. She had Bilal in his buggy, and Bilal was holding an envelope up to his nose and sniffing hard.

He always sniffs before he sucks, does Bilal.

Seeing Nani cheered us up, and when we heard what she had to say we were even more excited.

"Your dad was too late home last night to ask," she said, "so I had to wait till this morning."

She gave my arm a triumphant punch. "He's agreed!" she said. "The two of us can go to Thrill City for a night. That'll give us two whole days!"

She paused. "Just as long as you earn some money," she added. "Whatever you earn, he'll treble. Not bad, eh?"

I nodded. It wasn't bad. Treble is times three, so for every pound I earned, he'd make it up to £3.

And I'd never expected my dad just to let me go to Thrill City without some kind of fuss. He's into making me work for things I want. He says hard work never killed anyone, though I'm not sure if that's true.

"We've already started, Nani-jee," I said, gratefully heaving the metal detector into the buggy behind Bilal. "We're on a Treasure Quest."

"But we've only found 2p," Kylie said. "Which trebles up to 6p, I suppose," she added.

Nani looked over her glasses at us.

"You don't look dressed for a Treasure Quest," she said. "If you ask me, you look dressed for washing cars."

# Big Matt McBain

Washing cars didn't sound half as exciting as Treasure Questing. It certainly didn't sound like the kind of job Sita, Snake-Queen of Speed would stoop to. But then, Treasure Questing hadn't actually turned out to be very exciting, and, as Kylie pointed out, washing cars was much more likely to make us some money.

"And we do have the gloves for it," she added. "As your gran said."

So that's how we spent Saturday afternoon, and I'm telling you – it wasn't much fun, especially as I decided that if you needed one squirt of washing-up liquid for a bowlful of dishes, it followed that you'd need ten squirts for a car. Which was far too much, and it took us hours to get rid of the bubbles.

Then, when we were collecting the bucket and water at my house, Mum insisted we took Bilal. And she wouldn't let us take the buggy, because it was filthy after having the metal detector in it, so we had to carry him. He spent the whole afternoon sniffing around the bucket, and by the time Kylie and I realised that he was sniffing soap bubbles and then swallowing them, he had made himself sick.

By tea-time we were exhausted, so we set off for home, taking it in turns to carry Bilal who whimpered and dribbled down our backs the whole time. We were just about there when Kylie stopped and stared ahead with a worried expression. I stared too.

An enormous man was coming out of the allotment gate. He had a big bush of white hair, and big flappy trousers tied at the knees with string, and he was leading something that looked like a small brown tub with very thin legs, which turned out to be one of the ugliest dogs I'd ever seen.

It was extremely stout, and its skin was shiny and so tightly-stretched, it looked as if it might explode. Its bottom jaw jutted out so you could see a row of tiny, lethal-looking, yellow teeth, and its eye-sockets were so tight that its eyes were just two narrow, bloodshot slits. It wore a broad leather collar covered in metal spikes, and it looked like the Dog from Hell.

The man took great big steps, and the Dog from Hell

had to take about twenty steps to each of the man's. The nearer the man got, the huger he seemed, and the fiercer and more furious the dog.

"It's Big Matt McBain," Kylie whispered. "My dad's ferret-rival. You've got to watch him."

When Big Matt McBain reached us, he stopped and gave Kylie a big gummy grin. "Well now," he said, in a low, rumbly voice, "if it isn't Kylie Teasdale."

Kylie tried to walk on past, but Big Matt blocked her way. The Dog from Hell peered up at Bilal with its little red slit eyes, and whined. Bilal squirmed and screamed and wriggled in the dog's direction till Kylie put him down. Then the Dog from Hell and Bilal, who were roughly the same height when Bilal was sitting, stared silently at one another. Both were spellbound.

I didn't speak either. I just did what Kylie said, and watched Big Matt like anything. In particular, I watched Big Matt's big flappy trousers; and the more I watched, the odder I thought they were.

There was a strange, earthy smell coming from them, and, as if that wasn't enough, they were writhing.

Honestly. It was the weirdest thing – like ripples going up and down the left trouser leg.

Big Matt didn't seem at all fazed by his ripply trousers though. "Your dad all set for the Grand Ferret Championships next Saturday, lass?" he asked Kylie.

By this time, I wasn't the only one who was fascinated by the trouser legs. Bilal had crawled right up to them and was sniffing the left one with enormous interest.

"He sure is, Mr McBain," Kylie said carefully.

"Tell him I'll see him then," Big Matt said. Then he winked and added, "And his ferrets."

It wasn't a very friendly wink, somehow. I could see Kylie didn't like it either.

Then suddenly Big Matt frowned and looked down. "Leave off!" he shouted roughly at Bilal. "Me leg's all wet!"

"Sorry, Mr McBain," I said, and I pulled Bilal off and picked him up. The Dog from Hell peered at Bilal and gave a rather pathetic little whimper. When I looked back at the trousers, I saw there was a large damp patch on the left trouser leg. Bilal was licking his lips, and grinning from ear to ear.

Whatever was on Big Matt's trouser leg, it had fairly taken the taste of the soap bubbles away.

We walked on past as quickly as we could, and as soon as we did Bilal reached out his hands towards Big Matt, and screamed blue murder.

"What was in his trousers?" I asked Kylie, when we were out of earshot.

"Ferrets," Kylie explained. "Big Matt's got so many he hasn't room for them all at home. He keeps some of them on the allotment. He'll be taking them back with him to get them ready for the Grand Ferret Championship."

I could see Kylie was upset about meeting Big Matt McBain, so when we got home I gave Bilal back to Mum, and took Kylie upstairs to cheer her up by counting the money we'd earned.

It came to £2.50.

We tried to treble it in our heads, but it kept coming to £75 which we knew was too good to be true, so we went and asked Nani. Nani ran her tongue round her mouth several times and told us the answer was £7.50. And that meant that, altogether, Sita's Fearless Band of Snake-Warriors had earned £7.56. Which was, as Nani said, better than a kick in the teeth. But it wasn't enough to get us to Thrill City.

Kylie and I sat together on my bed, with Sita, Snake-Queen of Speed and the mongoose with its cobra, looking down at us; and we looked up at them, hoping for a flash of inspiration.

"That mongoose," Kylie said at last, "looks a bit like a ferret, don't you think?"

Then she sighed. "I do hope my dad wins Best in Show next Saturday, Yosser," she said. "He's been so close before, but somehow, Big Matt always manages to pip him at the post..."

I felt ever so sorry for her. She had ferrets on the brain.

Then I had an idea. "Tomorrow, Kylie," I said, putting my arm round her, "you can wear the yellow snake and be Sita, and I'll be the Humble Vassal, and we'll try somewhere else."

"Thanks Yosser," Kylie said, cheering up a little. "If we just keep looking, we're bound to find treasure in the end."

And, you know what, in the end we did. But it wasn't the kind of treasure we'd had in mind...

# An Absolute, Unmitigated Disaster

Next morning, when the doorbell rang, and I saw the blurred pink-and-orange outline of Kylie's head through the frosted glass, my first thought was, *Great – the Fearless Band of Snake-Warriors is making an early start.*

But the very instant I opened the door and saw Kylie's face, I knew something was wrong. Badly wrong.

"Oh Yosser!" she howled, throwing herself into my arms, "there's been an absolute, unmitigated disaster!"

"What on earth has happened?" I asked, but Kylie just kept hugging me, and sobbing on to my shoulder, and muttering *Thunderball... Thunderball... Thunderball* over and over again.

My stomach turned over. Somehow, even though the word *thunderball* meant nothing to me, I had an awful feeling I knew what the absolute, unmitigated disaster might be. I didn't want to start guessing, though, in case it wasn't.

I prised Kylie off my shoulder, took her arm very gently, like I do with Nani when her hip's playing up, and led her upstairs to my bedroom. I eased her down on to the bed and patted her head; and at last she stopped crying, took a long, wet, quivering breath, and spoke.

"It's Dad's prize Angora ferret," she said, very slowly and steadily, taking huge breaths in between each sentence. "Thunderball Silver the Third... the one that won Best in Class last year... the one who's bookies' favourite to win Best in Show this year..."

All the blood drained from my head. I'd been right. I knew what she was going to say next.

"When Dad went to check his cage this morning," Kylie whispered, "he'd gone."

Her eyes welled up with tears again and she stopped, sniffed, and rubbed her face with her sleeve.

"Dad's just devastated," she added, her voice muffled by sleeve and tears. Then she sat, staring blankly up in the direction of Sita, Snake-Queen of Speed, letting the rest of the tears plop down on to my duvet.

I couldn't think of anything to say just then, so I waited till Kylie felt able to go on, and as I waited I saw, as clear as day in my mind's eye, a big bush of white hair, a smelly, rippling trouser leg, and a wink you couldn't put your finger on.

"The lock on his cage had been tampered with," Kylie continued, her voice slightly stronger.

"He's been stolen," I said, and Kylie nodded.

"You bet your sweet life he's been stolen," she said. "And there's no prizes for guessing who's stolen him."

We sat in numb silence for a while, both thinking vicious thoughts about Big Matt McBain.

"But Kylie," I said after a bit, "I don't understand what good it'd do Big Matt to steal your dad's ferret. It's not as though he can do anything with him, because everyone knows who he belongs to."

Kylie gave me a pitying look. "You've no idea, Yosser," she said with a wry smile. "It's dog-eat-dog in the ferret world. If Big Matt's got Thunderball, then Thunderball can't win Best in Show, can he?"

I was about to tell Kylie that the Fearless Band of Snake-Warriors would stop at nothing to right this terrible wrong, when there was a little tap on the bedroom door. It opened a crack, and I saw the glint of Nani's glasses.

"Yosser ...may I come in?" she said.

"Sure," I said, and shuffled along the bed. Nani sat between me and Kylie, looked us both up and down, and then gave us each a hug.

"Not so good today?" she said quietly, and Kylie and me shook our heads and smiled bravely. I hoped Nani would think we were just upset about not finding treasure, and wouldn't ask any awkward questions. And, as it happened, she didn't.

As it happened, she had something else on her mind. And it was going to turn what was already a Very Bad Day into the Worst Day In Living Memory ...

"Your dad got a letter yesterday, Yosser," she said solemnly. "He was home too late to tell you about it, and he and your mum had to go to the fruit market early this morning, so they gave it to me to give you."

She pulled a piece of very thick, white, folded paper out of her sleeve and put it in my lap.

That Sunday must have been my day for being psychic, because I knew what the letter was about without even opening it. And, as I unfolded it, all the blood that had just newly gone back to my head drained away again.

At the top of the thick white paper, in big red letters, was 'OUR LADY OF THE SORROWS', and below it said:

Dear Mr and Mrs Farooq,

Re: Entrance exam, Yosser Farooq

I only read the first paragraph. I hadn't the heart to read any more. Then I sat very still, staring at the letter as if it was a death warrant; and, somewhere, far, far away in the distance, I heard my own voice saying *The entrance exam's on Friday. I am doomed.*

Which was the precise moment when the Worst Day In Living Memory began in earnest, and it led to the Worst Week in Living Memory.

# Desperate Measures

Nani gave me another hug, took the horrible letter out of my shaking hand, and shoved it back up her sleeve. Then she pointed a thumb at my Sita picture.

"Still keen to go, Yosser?" she asked.

It seemed like a funny question, but I looked up at Sita and her gleaming Snake Pod, and I thought about it. Stolen ferrets and entrance exams had put Thrill City right out of my head, but of course it was still there. I nodded at Nani, just out of politeness.

"Because if you are," Nani went on, and she wiggled her eyebrows up and down (which is Nani's sign that the next sentence contains Vital Information), "I'll just point out that if you pass the Entrance Exam with Distinction, you get a Bursary. Which means no fees."

She got up and headed for the door. Halfway out, she turned, nodded in the direction of Sita, and added, "Which means, I would have thought, a better bargaining position with You-Know-Who – wouldn't you?" And, with one last, enormous, wink, she was gone.

Kylie and me sat for a while, letting it all sink in. At last Kylie spoke.

"If I were you, Yosser," she said, "know what I'd do?"

"What?" I asked.

"I'd fail," Kylie said.

I gasped. "Really?" I said, and Kylie nodded.

"I know it's a desperate measure," she went on, "but if you go to Our Lady of the Sorrows, it's going to be awful. We've got to both go to Greater Malden Comprehensive."

I was horrified. Fail the Entrance Exam? Deliberately fail? I sat, stunned.

Then, just as I was about to tell Kylie I thought her plan was too dreadful for words, she jumped up, grabbed the plastic snakes off my bed-knob, wound the yellow one round her neck, and stood to attention.

"Come on, Yosser," she said, in a masterful voice. "There's no point sitting around all day worrying. There is a great wrong to be righted, and no time to lose."

Tossing the green plastic snake over to me, she added, "I'm Sita today, and you're the Humble Vassal, so I've decided to dispense with the gloves!"

And with that, she led the way down the stairs.

I followed Kylie out into the sunshine, and as soon as we were marching down the path I began to feel a whole lot better. I coiled my snake more tightly round my neck, so that I could see its yellow, glinting, snake-eyes, and I thought of the terrible thing Big Matt McBain had done; and the nearer we got to his house, the braver I felt.

"Right," said Kylie, stopping at a corner where a big privet hedge blocked our view, "we're getting close. We must proceed with caution."

And, keeping hard in to the hedge, she crept round the corner.

"On no account," she whispered, "must Spike get wind of us."

I gulped. Spike must be the name of the Dog from Hell, I realised, and there was no way on this earth I wanted him getting wind of me. I held my breath as we tiptoed along.

The big privet hedge seemed endless, but finally we reached a gate. The gate had a notice nailed to it, which said:

FIERCE GAURD DOG
KEEP OUT!

We looked over into Big Matt McBain's garden.

I could hardly believe my eyes. It looked like a rubbish dump! There were bits of old furniture, and car tyres, and broken beer barrels, lying all over the place, and in between grew long grass, and thistles, and nettles.

There was a path of sorts, that led past Big Matt's front door and on to another gate, and beyond that gate, partly hidden by bushes, were dozens and dozens of rusty, rickety cages. The cages were piled untidily one on top of each other. They were all painted in different colours, and the paint was faded and peeling.

"Wow!" I breathed. "What a mess!"

"It's a proper disgrace," muttered Kylie angrily. "And to think Thunderball Silver the Third could be in there!"

She sighed. "My dad keeps him in the most beautiful cage you could imagine. He'll not know what's hit him."

We stood, leaning on the gate, wondering how poor
Thunderball was coping with coming down in the
world.

"It's really quiet," I said after a while. "Maybe Big
Matt's out somewhere, with Spike..."

"Maybe he is," said Kylie, and she pushed the gate.
It opened with a loud creak, and as soon as it did, all hell
broke loose.

At first there was nothing to be seen. All we heard
was the most almighty, high-pitched roar coming from
somewhere in the long grass. Then we realised the roar

was getting louder and louder, and then, suddenly we saw a narrow channel in the grass that was getting closer by the second. It looked as though a very small, but very strong, tornado was hurtling towards us.

"Quick!" yelled Kylie, pushing me backwards and out on to the pavement again. In the nick of time, she slammed the gate shut.

Frozen in horror, we watched as Spike hurled his tight little body at the gate, growling and snarling and baring his evil yellow fangs at us, his bloodshot eyes glowing like the very Fires of Hell.

Then the front door was flung open and Big Matt's enormous form appeared on the doorstep. He was barefoot and wearing pyjama bottoms. His chest was bare except for a tattooed red heart with an arrow through it, and a thick growth of curly white hair. He shook his fist at Kylie and me.

"What the devil do yous think yous're doing?" he yelled at us. "Can't yous read?"

Kylie drew herself up as tall as she could, and gripped the yellow snake round her neck. She took a big breath, and when she spoke I was beside myself with admiration.

"Mr McBain, we have reason to suspect you are holding my dad's prize ferret against his will," she said, as calm and as steady as could be.

Big Matt's big mouth opened wide for a moment. Then he threw back his big head and howled with laughter. After a while he stopped. His smile faded clean away, and he glared at us as malevolently as I've ever been glared at. You could have cut the silence with a knife.

When he spoke again, his voice was low and grim.

"I'll tell you what, Kylie Teasdale," he growled, "if you say one thing to anyone about your dad's Thunderball, you'll wish you'd never been born ..."

He took a few steps along the path towards us, then thought better of it and retreated back into the doorway. Kylie opened her mouth and closed it again. She began to back away, pulling my arm.

"Yous have no proof! So make yourselves scarce," Big Matt yelled. "And if yous dare come nosing around, I'll set my dog on you!"

And with that he called Spike to heel, and the two disappeared into the house.

We made ourselves scarce as quickly as we could. We didn't stop running till we reached my street. Then we sat on the wall outside my house, and when we'd got our breath back we looked at one another in utter dismay. Our snakes suddenly looked very limp, and very plastic.

"Can't we go to the police?" I said.

"It's no good," said Kylie. "Big Matt's right. We've no proof."

We both sighed. It was true. You couldn't report someone to the police for having ripply trousers and a bad look in their eye. We sat in gloomy silence, considering the situation. The Grand Ferret Championship was six days away. My Entrance Exam for Our Lady of the Sorrows was five days away. Things couldn't have been more hopeless if they'd tried.

"It'll take more than a couple of plastic snakes to get us out of this mess," Kylie said at last, uncoiling hers and handing it sadly back to me.

And, as things turned out, in a way she was right. But, in another way, she was wrong.

# A Terrible, Tempting Idea

How Kylie and I got through the next week, I do not know.

Every day after school Kylie, armed with the yellow Sita-snake, would set off for another lonely vigil behind Big Matt McBain's privet hedge, hoping to catch sight of Thunderball Silver the Third. And every day I would set off home, armed with a load of worksheets from Ms Albright, for another exciting evening swotting maths and English Grammar.

By Thursday morning, we'd both hit rock bottom.

"Any luck last night?" I asked Kylie as she joined me on the wall outside the school. I knew from the way she'd been walking, with her head right down, that she hadn't had any luck, but I felt I had to ask anyway.

Kylie shook her head. "Not that I ever get close enough to see," she said, dismally.

"Doesn't Big Matt ever go out?" I asked.

I had a horrible picture in my head of Big Matt sitting by the window with a telescope trained on the gate, surrounded by enough boxes of food, drink and dog biscuits to last till the Grand Ferret Championship.

"Sure he goes out," Kylie said. "But he leaves

that vicious little hell-hound behind. He wasn't born yesterday."

I gave Kylie's arm a sympathetic squeeze, and agreed that he certainly wasn't.

"I don't know how he sleeps at night," I said. "He must have no conscience whatsoever."

Kylie nodded. "Completely unprincipled," she said. "How's the swotting?"

As soon as the word *swotting* was out, my stomach heaved and I felt sick.

I'd been feeling sick all week, actually, though that wasn't because of the swotting. I'm a bit shaky on maths, but I'm quite good at things like spelling and writing stories; so that wasn't the problem.

I wasn't feeling sick because of the thought of sitting the exam either, though it did scare me, particularly when I remembered Sister Mary Ignatius's huge eyes and thought of them watching me.

The sick feeling was because of something even worse. It was the idea – the terrible, tempting idea – that Kylie had given me, of failing the entrance exam. That was what made my stomach churn. I just couldn't think of anything else during the day, and even at night, when I managed to get to sleep, it haunted my dreams.

I knew it was an absolutely awful, dishonest thing to do. I knew it would hurt Mum and Dad like anything.

But I kept thinking how easy it would be to do it, and how, if I did do it, all my problems would be solved.

The way I saw it was this. If I passed the entrance exam, I'd have to spend the next six years in a red tartan uniform, working my socks off, without Kylie around. And since I probably wouldn't pass with Distinction and get a Bursary, because hardly anyone did, passing would also mean I wouldn't ever get to ride in Sita's Snake-Pod with Nani.

Sure, I'd make Mum and Dad happy, and I'd get my Hidden Potential unleashed. But it didn't seem like a fun way to do it.

If I failed, on the other hand, I could go to Great Malden Comprehensive, wear my combats to school, have Kylie there beside me all the way, and, as like as not, unleash my Hidden Potential into the bargain.

And, when I thought about it like that, there didn't seem much choice.

"The swotting's fine," I told Kylie. "But I've decided to fail."

Kylie stared at me. "You haven't!" she gasped.

I stared back at her, wondering why on earth she was so shocked. "But Kylie," I said, "it was your idea! Why're you looking at me like that?"

Kylie bit her lip, and so did I. After all, I'd expected her to be pleased.

"I just didn't think you'd do it," she said. "I felt bad afterwards for even suggesting it. Somehow I didn't think being dishonest was your 'thing'..."

At that point the bell rang and we slipped down off the wall and began to walk to the lines. As we arrived Ms Albright, who had bought herself a little whistle, was blowing very loudly and shrilly at the football stragglers.

"I have to fail," I whispered to Kylie above the racket. "I can't go it alone for the next six years..."

Ms Albright, her face extremely red, stopped whistling to draw breath. Hastily, I zipped my mouth and placed a finger on my lips, and Kylie did the same.

At Ms Albright's signal, we all began to shuffle towards the door.

"Yosser..." Kylie hissed, being careful not to move

her finger.

"What?" I said.

"I just wanted to say," she whispered, "that even if

you don't fail, and you do go to Our Lady of the Sorrows, you won't go it alone." She shot a quick glance over her shoulder. "Because wherever you are, I'll always be there for you."

Which is the nicest thing anyone ever said to me.

# The Entrance Exam

Remember that feeling I told you about, that's like an electric current rushing up your back?

Well, there is a feeling that's opposite to that one. It feels like everything in your whole body is sinking into your feet, and on the way down it's making your stomach do back-flips and your legs wobble. It's the most horrible feeling there is, and it's the feeling I got when Mum dropped me off at Our Lady of the Sorrows for my Entrance Exam.

All the way there I'd sat in the back of the car, between Nani and Bilal, not saying a word. And I'd cuddled Bilal like anything, and wished we'd never, ever arrive.

But of course we did, and as I got out everyone gave me a kiss (actually, Bilal's kiss was more of a Sniff-n-Suck, but it was greatly appreciated), and Nani pressed something small and soft into my hand.

"Good luck, Yosser," she said. "And don't be afraid to use it!" she added.

Then Mum pressed the accelerator hard and they zoomed off, leaving me all alone with only the horrible sinking feeling, and the small soft thing, for company.

I climbed the steps to the main entrance, and as I did

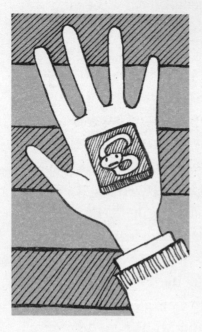

I opened my hand and looked at Nani's present. It was a green rubber with a yellow snake on it.

Sister Mary Ignatius was waiting in the entrance hall. There was another nun standing beside her, who was quite young and very big. The big nun had the widest smile, and the sparkliest blue eyes, I'd ever seen.

"Come along, Yosser," said Sister Mary Ignatius. "Best foot forward." And she led the way to the hall, which was bursting at the seams with girls. All the girls were sitting at desks with their pencils poised – and none of them looked as terrified as I was.

The first paper was maths. Now, I'd spent the last week thinking out my Failing Strategy, so I knew just what I was going to do. There was no point, I reckoned, in just writing down rubbish answers. That would only arouse suspicion.

No, I knew my Failing Strategy would only work if I

calculated the correct answer and then put down an answer that was just slightly wrong. Which was a bit of a pain, because it meant I actually had to do a whole load of work for nothing.

"Pick up your pencils, girls," Sister Mary Ignatius said, in her quiet, determined voice, "and begin."

I read the first question, and was quite surprised. I'd expected, given that maths isn't my strong point, to find the sums impossible. But actually they weren't. I pretty well sailed through them, working them out on scrap paper and then writing down wrong answers on the sheet.

But as I did, a strange thing began to happen. Every time I wrote down a wrong answer I had this uncanny feeling that Sister Mary Ignatius' big black eyes were on me, watching what I was up to. I kept looking at her, and every time I did, I'll swear she was looking straight at me. And given there must have been about a hundred girls in that hall – was that spooky or what?

Then another strange thing happened. I started to have visions, in my head. Not holy visions of angels or anything. Unholy visions of Big Matt McBain, with his shock of white hair and his wink that you couldn't put your finger on.

Big Matt McBain, who'd ferret-napped Kylie's dad's

precious Thunderball Silver the Third so he could win Best in Show.

Big Matt McBain, the most despicable, dishonourable man on Planet Earth.

And then I pictured my mum and dad, hard at work in Farooq's Fruits. And I could just see Dad, so worried about how I was doing that he'd be giving everyone the wrong change; and Mum, telling every single customer that her little girl was sitting the most important exam of her life. And I saw Nani, taking an oven-glove out of Bilal's mouth, and saying a little prayer to help me.

Then I pictured myself, writing down all these wrong answers even though I knew what the right answers were. And suddenly I had the most awful thought I have ever had... I was just as bad as Big Matt McBain. I was as much of a cheat. I was every bit as dishonourable.

A tear trickled down my cheek and I reached for the rubber Nani had given me, and know what? As if by magic, Sister Mary Ignatius was standing right beside me. And as I picked up the rubber and began to rub out my wrong answers, she put her hand on my head and, when I looked up at her, she gave me a huge, magnified wink!

And, also as if by magic, the horrible sinking feeling I'd had all week vanished into thin air.

There was a big clock on the wall above me and I

could see I had just enough
time to correct the wrong
answers and finish the paper.
As soon as I had, Sister Mary
Ignatius gathered in the maths
paper, and gave us the English
one. Which was no problem,
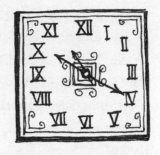
because you had to write an essay called *What I Look
For in a Friend*, so naturally I wrote all about Kylie and
what made her special.

As I was writing about Kylie, I started to feel a bit
bad again. I was pretty sure I'd pass and get in to Our
Lady of the Sorrows, and that would mean not going
with Kylie to Great Malden Comprehensive. But then I
remembered what Kylie had said – that wherever I was,
she'd always be there for me. And I wrote that down at
the end of my essay.

It was a perfect way to end, and it made me feel a
whole lot better. And I knew that later, when I explained
to Kylie that I hadn't failed, she'd understand.

I thought the exam was finished then, but it wasn't.
Sister Mary Ignatius told us that Sister Felicity would
take us in groups to the Art Room, and the big smily
nun told my row to follow her.

I just couldn't believe it. And when I saw Sister
Felicity's Art Room, that electric current didn't half zip

up my back and make my entire body tingle!

It was out-of-this-world amazing. There was every kind of paint you could ever have wished for, in great big pots so you didn't have to worry about using too much. There was clay, and plaster, and wire for making statues. There was wool, and thread, and sequins for doing collages. There were bales and bales of the most wonderful bright material to do fashion design with. There was wood, and chisels, and saws, and knives for carving. And every bit of the walls was covered with fabulous pictures that other children had done.

Sister Felicity showed us where to sit, and she gave us enormous pieces of paper.

"Paint what inspires you, girls!" she told us. "Paint your greatest dream!"

Well, I didn't have to think about it for even a second. I took a piece of charcoal from the table, and I drew a big picture of Sita, Snake-Queen of Speed.

I drew her dress with flames leaping up from its hem. I drew her snakeskin gloves, and her snakeskin boots, and the golden snake round her neck. I made her muscles bulge as she pointed to her Snake-Pod, and, in the Snake-Pod, I drew Nani and me. I also drew Kylie in the Snake-Pod, even though she wasn't coming, because it was a picture of my greatest dream.

I wished I could draw the Truly Massive G-Force, but

I still couldn't.

It did occur to me, though, that Sister Mary Ignatius was just the kind of woman who'd know what a Truly Massive G-Force was...

Finally, I drew Sita's hair with a whole load of snakes writhing about in it.

When I'd finished painting my picture, I really thought it was the best one I'd ever done, and when I handed it to Sister Felicity, I distinctly heard her mutter *Wow!* under her breath.

So I knew she thought the same.

# Bilal Saves The Day

Next morning, before Mum, Nani, Bilal and I had even finished breakfast, Kylie rang the doorbell, and when I opened the door she gave me a hug and a bright congratulations-on-surviving-the-Entrance-Exam smile.

I could see behind the smile, though. Kylie's eyes had dark circles under them and her hair was spiky in all the wrong places. I knew she was feeling terrible. I also knew that, with the Grand Ferret Championship set to start in less than four hours, there was only the slimmest of chances we'd find Thunderball Silver the Third in time.

But I also knew that, when Kylie and me became the Fearless Band of Snake-Warriors, we could do things that were impossible to do on our own. And, when the chips were down, we had to have one last go at Righting the Great Wrong.

"How's your dad?" I said, leading the way upstairs.

"He's making the best of it," she said, following me. "But his heart's not in it."

We knotted the snakes round our necks. Kylie took the yellow one again, and I let her. I knew she needed to feel like Sita, today of all days. Then we did our Snake-Warrior salute and set off for Big Matt McBain's house as quickly as we could.

We didn't set off quickly enough to avoid Mum, who made me take Bilal because he'd been crying all morning and giving Nani a headache. And Bilal howled and dribbled all the way to Big Matt McBain's gate.

We stood, quaking, for a while. And then we realised that Bilal had stopped howling. He was listening, with a big smile on his face, to a low, rumbling growl far off in the distant wilderness of Big Matt's garden.

Kylie looked at me, and I looked at Kylie. She was deathly pale, but her eyes glowed bright.

"It's our last chance to rescue Thunderball," she said grimly, pushing the gate open. "We're going in."

Cautiously, we slipped through. Spike's terrible rumbling seemed to make even the tips of the long grass vibrate.

"Think of it as a dragon roaring," I whispered.
"Sita would make mincemeat of a dragon!"

Slightly comforted, we began to pick our way along
the path in between the rubbish. Then we reached the
second gate, that led into Big Matt's back garden.

It had a notice on it too, which said:

...which didn't exactly cheer us up.

Suddenly the rumbling growl changed into a volley of
barks, and Big Matt, with Spike on the lead, rose out of
the long grass with a bucket in his hand and a furious
scowl on his face. They both hurtled towards us.

I turned to leave, but I didn't get far because when
Bilal saw Big Matt, he wriggled out of my arms and,
before I could grab him, he ran towards the gate with
very wobbly, but very fast, steps.

His first steps.

Then he fell against the gate with such a bang that it
opened. And before you could say *spitting cobras*, he was
sniffing at Big Matt's trouser legs, and Spike, who'd
slipped his spiky collar, was running towards him as fast
as his skinny legs would let him.

I don't think I've ever felt as scared. I had this terrible picture in my head of Spike sinking his sharp yellow teeth into Bilal, just like Nani's mongoose. For a moment I closed my eyes, and the next thing I remember seeing was Spike licking the side of Bilal's head as if he'd found a long-lost friend.

I was so relieved! Not that being licked by a dog with yellow teeth is the best thing for a toddler, but compared to being savaged to death, it's a picnic.

Big Matt McBain, meanwhile, looked as if he'd explode with rage.

"I ain't got your dad's flipping ferret!" he bellowed at us. "So get lost!"

I slipped through the gate and began to haul Bilal away from the trouser leg, but Spike snarled at me so I stopped. I couldn't have budged Bilal anyway. He clung like a limpet, sniffing and sucking at the string that was tied near the ankle. And that trouser leg was writhing like it had never writhed before.

Then, quite suddenly and unexpectedly, Bilal bit through the string and it fell off. Like a bright little river, a long thin flash of silvery-white poured out of the bottom of Big Matt's trouser leg.

Kylie yelled "Thunderball!" at the top her voice, and went charging through the long grass, jumping over empty beer barrels and weaving her way in between

clumps of thistles and ferret cages. Every now and then, Kylie would make a dive for Thunderball, but he was far too fast and silky-slippery for her.

Spike was chasing after Thunderball too, though we couldn't see him. We could just hear lots of little high-pitched yelps. And Bilal was howling, and Big Matt McBain was stamping through the grass behind Kylie shouting, "I only borrowed him, honest!"

So it was hardly surprising that no one saw me pick Bilal up, and give him a cuddle, and say, "Wow! You cut your first tooth!"

After a while, Kylie gave up chasing Thunderball and Big Matt gave up chasing Kylie, and they came stomping back to the gate, shouting at one another.

"I'll have you know, Mr McBain," Kylie was yelling, "that there's a law against borrowing ferrets!"

I couldn't believe how strong and fearless Kylie was, standing up to Big Matt McBain like that. The streaks in her hair looked like lots of tiny snakes, and the yellow rubber snake round her neck glowed in the sun, like gold. Also, I hadn't known there was a law against borrowing ferrets, so I was dead impressed that Kylie did.

Big Matt McBain looked down at his big boots, and his face went very red.

"I didn't mean no harm, lass," he muttered. "I'd 'ave

given 'im back..."

But Kylie was having none of it.

"We've got two hours to catch Thunderball," she told him, "or there will be Big Trouble."

Big Matt, looking extremely humble, got a bag and a pole, and set off to try. Kylie and I sat on a car tyre and watched him.

"It's no good, Yosser," Kylie said, after about half an hour. "Thunderball isn't called Thunderball for nothing. He's the fastest ferret in Yorkshire."

I wanted to say something to cheer her up, but I couldn't, so I changed the subject.

"Good about Bilal's tooth, isn't it?" I said. "If he hadn't bitten through the string, we'd never have found Thunderball."

"Great," said Kylie, doing her best to sound enthusiastic. "Now maybe he'll stop sucking things..."

We both looked over at Bilal. He was leaning happily against Spike, making smacking noises with his lips.

"Funny he hasn't talked yet..." Kylie said thoughtfully.

In the distance the Town Hall clock struck twelve.

"Dad'll be arriving with his ferrets," Kylie sighed. "But in the spot that's reserved for Thunderball Silver the Third, there will be an empty cage."

I leant over and gave Kylie's back a pat. And it was as

75

I leant over that I saw I was being watched.

A few metres away, from inside a tunnel of car tyres, two bright black eyes stared out at me. I nudged Kylie.

"Oh Yosser," Kylie whispered, gripping my arm hard.

For when our eyes got used to the dark, we could see that those deep black starry-bright eyes were twinkling in a sky of silvery-white fur.

# Sita, Snake-Queen of Speed

Don't make any sudden movements," Kylie whispered.

We sat as still as stuffed mongooses, staring at Thunderball's bright eyes. And Thunderball, safe inside his car-tyre tunnel, stared back at us.

"Can't you call him to heel?" I asked.

Kylie shook her head, and my heart sank. At this rate, we could be sitting in Big Matt's garden staring at Thunderball till next year's Grand Ferret Championships.

But we were saved from that. We were saved, because at that moment Bilal said his first word – and a very odd word it was.

"Nake."

Hardly believing our ears, we turned to look at him.

"Nake!" he repeated, more loudly.

"What's he saying?" Kylie hissed. "He's going to scare Thunderball..."

"Nake!" Bilal shouted again, at the top of his voice. "Nake! Nake! NAKE!"

He bounced up and down, waving his hands in Kylie's direction.

I looked over at what Bilal was pointing at, and suddenly it all came clear. And I realised that my baby brother Bilal was not only able to walk, chew, and speak...

My baby brother Bilal was a genius!

There was no time to lose. Carefully I pulled the yellow plastic snake from Kylie's neck. Kylie wrinkled her brow, but there was no time for explanations. The Humble Vassal was taking charge.

I crept up to the car tyre tunnel with the snake. Thunderball stared out at me. I prayed he wouldn't back away.

He didn't. He crept forward. Soon he was close enough for me to see his nose. It was sniffing excitedly.

Kylie had cottoned on by that time. "Make it writhe," she whispered.

I gave the snake a shake. It writhed ever so realistically, and Thunderball sniffed faster.

"Writhe it a bit more..." Kylie said.

I gave three enormous writhes, and on the third one, Thunderball raced toward the snake and pounced.

He hurled himself onto it, and I let go. Then he bit it over and over again, making furious spitting noises as he tumbled about, wrapping the snake round and round himself.

Big Matt and Bilal and Spike had joined us by then, and we all watched as Thunderball tore the plastic snake limb from limb. Except snakes haven't got any limbs, but you know what I mean.

Then Thunderball, his mouth spattered with foamy white spit, reared up above what was left of the snake. He looked quite noble, in a vicious, ferrety sort of way, and more like Nani's stuffed mongoose than ever.

But his moment of glory didn't last. Before he had the chance to lunge down for the final kill, Big Matt threw a sack over him, scooped him up, and tied a knot. Then he handed the sack to Kylie.

"May the best ferret win, lass," he said quietly.

Then he walked over to one of his cages, stuck a finger in, and began, very gently, to stroke a pink quivering nose.

"He'll never show ferrets again," Kylie whispered as I picked Bilal up and we made our way out of the garden. "Never."

"Quite right too," I whispered back.

And so it was. The Fearless Band of Snake Warriors had Righted the Great Wrong.

All the same though, I knew it would be a long time before I forgot the look on Big Matt McBain's face as he stroked that pink, quivering, nose...

★ ★ ★

Kylie and me ran like the wind to the Town Hall, which was difficult because Kylie had a sackful of writhing Thunderball, and I had an armful of screaming Bilal. We tumbled up the steps just in time to hear the judge announce, "And now – the moment you've all been waiting for..."

"There's your dad, Kylie!" I said, pulling her over to a table where her dad was standing, surrounded by ferret-cages. He looked more miserable than I've ever seen anyone look, ever.

"This year," the judge was saying, "the Best In Show prize of £500 goes to..."

He paused. I braced myself.

"Wait!" I shouted. I ran right up to the judge, who stopped and looked over his specs at me.

"Please, your honour," I said, as politely as I could, "there's a Late Entry."

You could have heard a ferret-whisker quiver in the

silence that fell over that hall. Kylie tipped the sack on to her dad's table, and Thunderball Silver the Third, covered in what looked like yellow confetti, tumbled out.

The moment his feet hit the table he stood, like the champion ferret he was, with his legs straight and his silky-white tail stretched out behind him like a magnificent plume, and Kylie's dad, his mouth wide open, gaped at him in utter, delighted, astonishment.

He stroked him from nose to tail, removing the last of the plastic snake-bits, and muttered lovingly, "Me little Treasure... me little Treasure..."

The judge marched to the table, and Kylie cupped her hand and whispered in his ear for ages. When she had finished, he straightened up and gave her an understanding nod.

Then he pushed and prodded Thunderball like anything. He peered into his eyes and he peered into his mouth. He even lifted up his tail and peered into his bottom. And when he had finished, he walked back to the stage and said:

"It is my pleasure to announce this year's Best In Show – Stanley Teasdale's Thunderball Silver the Third!"

As Kylie's dad made his way to the stage, he could hardly get through the crowd of clapping, cheering people. When he did, and the judge presented him with the big bundle of prize money, he had tears streaming down his face.

And when he handed us each a £20 note, Kylie and me thought we would die of happiness.

Then Kylie looked down to the floor where Bilal was sitting. He was in his own little world, breathing in the wonderful ferrety smells all around him.

"It'd take too long to explain just now," she whispered to her dad, "but actually, it was Bilal who got Thunderball back."

Her Dad gave her a funny look, and then he smiled.

"Well, in that case," he said, handing Bilal another £20 note, "he'll be wanting one of these too, won't he!"

I thanked Kylie's dad and removed the £20 note before it hit Bilal's mouth. Then I picked him up, and wiped him down, and we walked home, doing mental maths like mad.

"Altogether," I told Kylie after a while, "I reckon we've got £47.56."

"Which is nearly £50," Kylie pointed out. "Which, trebled... is..."

"... enough to go to Thrill City, I'll bet!" I said.

"And I'll tell you something else, Kylie," I added. "If Nani and me go, you've got to come too. Think your mum and dad'll let you?"

* * *

Nani and I did go to Thrill City. And of course Stanley Teasdale, Ferret Champion of Yorkshire, let Kylie go too.

We got to go for two nights, too, in a brilliant hotel with a pool and a jacussi, and that was because I not only passed my entrance exam to Our Lady of the Sorrows, I won the Bursary. When Sister Mary Ignatius phoned, she told us there had been extremely stiff competition, and that I'd done really well in maths and English, but what had clinched it was my painting. My painting of Sita, Snake-Queen of Speed!

So I suppose you could say that it was Sita herself who took us to Thrill City; and, believe me, Thrill City was absolutely, mind-blowingly, fantastic.

As soon as we got into the park, we could see Sita. She was huge, and, just like Kylie had said, she moved, and the snakes in her head writhed about, and when they opened their jaws you could actually see drips of deadly venom and blood.

And when she said, in her wonderful, hissy voice, *I am S-s-s-s-s-s-s-sita, S-s-s-s-s-s-s-s-s-snake-Queen of S-s-s-s-s-s-s-s-s-speed. Do you dare to ride with me?"* I thought I'd go up in smoke, because that electric

current zinged up my back like never before.

In fact, though I know Sita isn't really real, I reckon when she said, *Do you dare to ride with me?* she looked straight into my eyes.

And when I said, "You bet your life I dare!", I'd swear she gave a little smile right in my direction!

Then we got strapped into a Snake Pod, and we each held a bloodstained fang (which wasn't wet and sticky with blood, and maybe that was just as well) and we rode with Sita seventeen times. At least, Kylie and me rode with her seventeen times. Nani decided after the first time that it had been great, but that she'd be quite happy eating candy floss and drinking cappuccinos for the rest of the day. That way, she explained, she wouldn't have to take off her glasses, and take out her teeth, and put them in a plastic bag...

Which brings me to the Truly Massive G-Force.

Now, to understand a Truly Massive G-Force, you really have to experience it for yourself. But, in case you never do, this is what it's like. When a Truly Massive G-Force hits you, it feels as if the earth's gravity suddenly got a hundred times stronger, and instead of just keeping your feet stuck down on to the ground, it sticks everything down. Your cheeks are sucked in, and your ears are sucked in, and your tummy's sucked in. Even your eyes are sucked in, so they feel they might pop right into your brain and get the closest look ever at your Hidden Potential.

It is thoroughly, totally awesome.

Of course, we didn't take Bilal with us. We left him to eat Auntie Rosina's table-legs. But we put his £20 in a safe place, and Dad promised that every year he'd double it, so when Bilal is bigger he'll take us all to Thrill City and we'll ride with Sita again.

Because, you know, everyone should ride with Sita,

Snake-Queen of Speed. Everyone should get strapped into a Snake Pod, and hold on to a bloodstained fang, and get propelled by a Truly Massive G-force into Sita's Snake-Kingdom for the Thrill Ride to end all Thrill Rides, once in their lives.

Everyone.

**FRANZESKA G. EWART** began her career
teaching Biology, and later taught English
as an Additional Language. She taught in Karachi,
Pakistan, and while she was there, used shadow
puppets in language development. She often uses
shadow puppetry to help people express themselves,
and has written several books on the subject.
She lives in the village of Lochwinnoch, in Scotland,
where she enjoys the countryside and wildlife.
Her other book for Frances Lincoln is
*There's a Hamster in my Pocket*.

## MORE LAUGH-OUT-LOUD FICTION FROM FRANCES LINCOLN CHILDREN'S BOOKS

### THERE'S A HAMSTER IN MY POCKET!
Franzeska G. Ewart
Illustrated by Helen Bate

Yosser's having a very worrying summer.
Auntie Shabnam's coming to save the family shop,
so Yosser's going to have to share a room with Nani
and her creepy stuffed animals. . .
Yosser's best friend Kylie's got problems too – huge
problems, in the shape of her big brother Sniper
and his rapper mates. When Yosser discovers
a mysterious box among Nani's things, she suspects
it is at the root of all the bad luck.
Can she solve the mystery of the locked wooden box,
get to the bottom of Sniper's strange behaviour,
find the perfect present for Kylie's mum . . .
and all without losing the hamsters?

## PURPLE CLASS AND THE SKELINGTON
### Sean Taylor
### Illustrated by Helen Bate

Meet Purple Class – there is Jamal who often forgets
his reading book, Ivette who is the best in the class
at everything, Yasmin who is sick on every school trip,
Jodie who owns a crazy snake called Slinkypants,
Leon who is great at rope-swinging, Shea who knows
all about blood-sucking slugs and Zina who makes a rather
disturbing discovery in the teacher's chair...

Has Mr Wellington died? Purple Class is sure he must
have done when they find a skeleton sitting in his chair.
Is this Mr Wellington's skelington? What will they say
to the school inspector? Featuring a calamitous cast
of classmates, the adventures of Purple Class
will make you laugh out loud in delight.

## PURPLE CLASS AND THE FLYING SPIDER
Sean Taylor
Illustrated by Helen Bate

Purple Class are back in four new school stories!
Leon has managed to lose 30 violins, much to the horror
of the violin teacher; Jodie thinks she has uncovered
an unexploded bomb in the vegetable patch;
Shea has allowed Bad Boy, Purple Class's guinea pig
to escape; and Ivette has discovered a scary flying spider,
just in time for Parent's Evening!

## PURPLE CLASS
## AND THE HALF-EATEN SWEATER
Sean Taylor
Illustrated by Helen Bate

Mr Wellington's precious cricket sweater is in the bin,
Shea and Jamal have to do a half-hour sponsored silence,
Jodie says there's a werewolf on the class trip,
and Ivette's surprise birthday cake gets sat on.
Four crazy stories about the funniest class ever.

"Crammed full of zany and exuberant characters
and the mishaps and mayhem that ensue."
Jake Hope, *Achuka*

## WASIM AND THE WANDERER
Chris Ashley
Illustrated by Kate Pankhurst

No one at school can score a goal like Wasim!
So he is trying out his football skills for
Teamwork 10,000 and that might just lead to
a trial with the Woodley Wanderers!
But how can he play his best football
with Robert Bailey lurking around
every corner – and then on
the football pitch too?

## WASIM'S CHALLENGE
Chris Ashley
Illustrated by Kate Pankhurst

Wasim's class are off to Snowdonia on a
Challenge by Choice week and he can't wait!
And that's not the only challenge Wasim is facing –
this year he has secretly decided to fast for Ramadan
for the first time. But as usual, nothing goes right
for Wasim, and when a box of Mars bars disappears,
he becomes prime suspect.
Can he prove his innocence and meet his challenges?